Honey Hunt

By Barbara Diamond
Illustrated by John and Alexandra Wallner

Mary wanted honey.
But the honey was
almost gone!

She put
some honey
in a dish.

She put
some water
in the dish.

She put the dish
in the grass.

Buzz! Buzz!
Look at the dish.

Buzz! Buzz!
Look at the bee.

Buzz! Buzz!
Look at the tree.
Look at the honey tree!

Now Mary can tell Mama
where to get more honey.